W9-DBZ-348

ONLY SIX MORE DAYS

by Marisabina Russo

Puffin Books

PUFFIN BOOKS
Published by the Penguin Group
Viking Penguin, a division of Penguin Books USA Inc.,
375 Hudson Street, New York, New York 10014, U.S.A.
Penguin Books Ltd, 27 Wrights Lane, London W8 5TZ, England
Penguin Books Australia Ltd, Ringwood, Victoria, Australia
Penguin Books Canada Ltd, 10 Alcorn Avenue, Toronto, Ontario, Canada M4V 3B2
Penguin Books (N.Z.) Ltd, 182–190 Wairau Road, Auckland 10, New Zealand

Penguin Books Ltd, Registered Offices: Harmondsworth, Middlesex, England

First published in the United States of America by Greenwillow Books,
a division of William Morrow & Company, 1988
Reprinted by arrangement with William Morrow & Company, Inc.
Published in Puffin Books, 1992
1 3 5 7 9 10 8 6 4 2
Copyright © Marisabina Russo Stark, 1988
All rights reserved

LIBRARY OF CONGRESS CATALOGING-IN-PUBLICATION DATA
Russo, Marisabina.
Only six more days / by Marisabina Russo.   p.   cm.
Summary: Becoming more and more annoyed as her brother Ben counts
down the days until his birthday, Molly considers refusing to take
part in the celebration.
ISBN 0-14-054473-9
[1. Birthdays—Fiction.   2. Brothers and sisters—Fiction.]
I. Title.   II. Title: Only 6 more days.
[PZ7.R9192On   1992]   [E]—dc20   91-29565

Printed in Hong Kong
Set in Kabel Book

Except in the United States of America, this book is sold subject
to the condition that it shall not, by way of trade or otherwise,
be lent, re-sold, hired out, or otherwise circulated without the
publisher's prior consent in any form of binding or cover other than
that in which it is published and without a similar condition including
this condition being imposed on the subsequent purchaser.

FOR

SUSAN,

LIBBY,

AND

AVA

Ben counted the days until his birthday.
"Only six more days!" said Ben.
"Who cares?" said his sister Molly. And
    she pretended to feed Katie some cereal.

When there were only five more days, Ben said,
"Hooray! Everyone I invited can come to my party:
Kevin, Daniel, Joey, and Matthew."
"Only boys?" said Molly. "Yuck."

The next day, when Molly came home
from school, Ben met her at the door.
"Look at my party favors," he said.
"So what," said Molly.
"Only four more days," said Ben.

When there were only three more days left,
Ben and his father made a list of party games.
Ben wanted Duck Duck Goose.
"Oh, that's a baby game," said Molly.

Two days before his birthday, Ben
decided to clean up his room.
He cleared off one shelf of his bookcase.
"Why are you doing that?" asked Molly.
"So I have a place for all my presents,"
 said Ben.
"What if you only get socks?" said Molly.

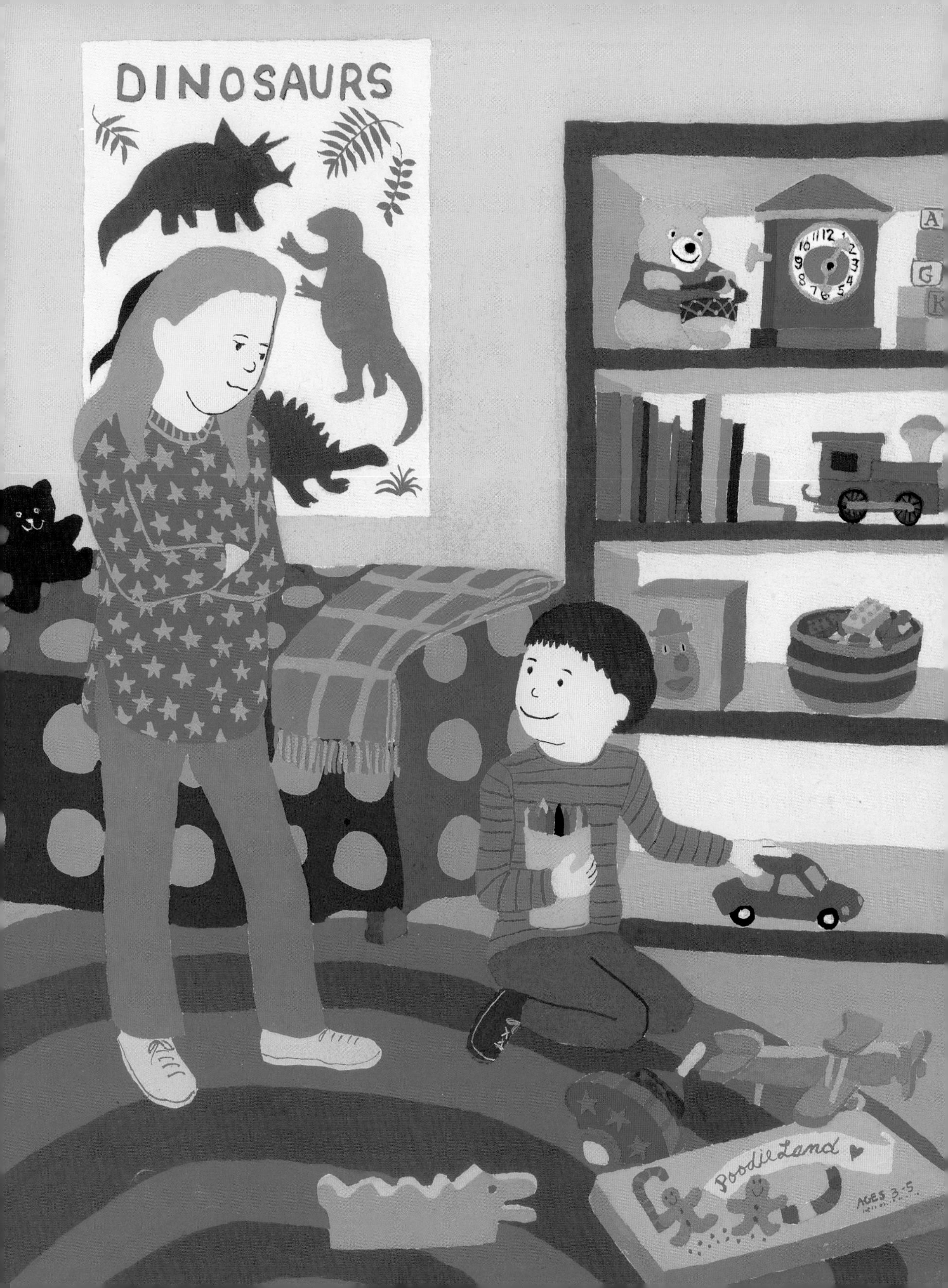
DINOSAURS
PoodleLand
AGES 3-5

One day before Ben's birthday his
mother baked a chocolate cake.
Ben licked the bowl clean before
Molly got home from school.
When Molly saw the cake she said,
"Chocolate! My doll Katie hates
chocolate."

On the day of his birthday
Ben announced,

"Hooray, hooray,
I'm five today!
I'll never be four again!"

"Thank goodness!" said Molly.

"Happy birthday," said his mother.
"Happy birthday," said his father.
Molly sat silently. Her mother and
father looked at her.

"Happy birthday, Ben," said Molly
finally. "Oh, by the way, I can't
come to your party."

"Why not?" asked Ben.

"I just remembered that today is Katie's
birthday, too, and since she is my favorite
baby I have to give her a party," said Molly.

"You're going to miss something great,"
said Ben.

Molly went upstairs to her room. Her mother
came to the door.
"Molly, Ben is really disappointed that you
can't come to his party."
"Oh sure," said Molly.
"Couldn't you have Katie's party when Ben's
party is over?" her mother asked.

"I'm sick and tired of Ben's birthday," said
   Molly. "It's all anybody ever talks about."
   Molly's mother walked over to the wall.
   She took down the calendar and flipped
   a couple of pages. She showed Molly
   something.
   Molly smiled.
"Now get yourself ready for Ben's party,"
   said her mother.

When Ben's friends began to arrive, Molly
came downstairs with Katie.

"What about Katie's party?" said Ben.

"Oh, we'll have it a little later," said Molly.

"A girl?" said Daniel. "Pee-uuu!"

"Molly's no girl. She's my sister," said Ben.

When it was time to open the presents,
Molly hid hers behind her back.
She wanted Ben to open it last.

Ben got a robot, a fire truck, a game, and a pair of finger puppets. He got an easel from his mother and father.

"Here, Ben," said Molly at last.

"Oh boy, another present!" said Ben. Inside he found a gum wrapper chain, two baseball cards, Molly's old roller skates, and a letter.

"This stuff is neat," said Ben.

"Read the letter," said Molly.

"You know I can't read," said Ben.

"I'll read it," said Molly. "It says—

Dear Ben,
I'm happy today is your birthday because now we don't have to count the days to your birthday any more. Now we can start counting the days to my birthday.
Love,
Molly
P.S. Only 47 more days!